THE MISSING RIDER

Corey settled into her saddle and began her warm-up circles around the ring.

"All right," Max called. "Now that we're all here, come on over and let me tell you what our program will be."

Now that we're all here. Max's words rang in Corey's ears. They weren't all there. Jasmine was still missing.

Quickly Corey counted the other riders.

Then Corey understood. Jasmine wasn't in the small group.

Corey had been chosen and Jasmine hadn't!

Jasmine's Christmas Ride

BONNIE BRYANT

Illustrated by Marcy Ramsey

A SKYLARK BOOK
NEW YORK • TORONTO • LONDON • SYDNEY • AUCKLAND

RL3 007–010
JASMINE'S CHRISTMAS RIDE
A Skylark Book / November 1995

*Skylark Books is a registered trademark of Bantam Books,
a division of Bantam Doubleday Dell Publishing Group, Inc.
Registered in U.S. Patent and Trademark Office and elsewhere.
Pony Tails is a trademark of Bonnie Bryant Hiller.*

ISBN 0-553-48258-0

Published simultaneously in the United States and Canada

*Bantam Books are published by Bantam Books, a division of Bantam
Doubleday Dell Publishing Group, Inc. Its trademark, consisting of the words
"Bantam Books" and the portrayal of a rooster, is Registered in U.S. Patent
and Trademark Office and in other countries. Marca Registrada. Bantam
Books, 1540 Broadway, New York, New York 10036.*

PRINTED IN THE UNITED STATES OF AMERICA

0   9   8   7   6   5   4   3   2   1

Jasmine's
Christmas Ride

1 Pony Tails in the Ring

"There! I felt another one!" Jasmine James cried, looking at the sky. "It's snowing! I'm sure of it. We're going to have a white Christmas this year!"

Jasmine and her two best friends, Corey Takamura and May Grover, were all riding their ponies. They were in the practice ring behind May's house. They were trying to work on the exercises they'd learned at their Pony Club meeting the day before. But it was hard to concentrate on perfect riding form when Christmas was less than two weeks away.

May looked up at the sky, too. She wasn't as sure as Jasmine about the snow. She stuck out her tongue to try to catch a flake.

"Nothing," she announced. "Not yet."

1

"You're just not patient enough," Jasmine told her. "It *is* snowing. I'm sure."

"Even if it snows now," Corey reminded them, "the snow might be gone when we go on that Christmas Eve ride—what's it called?"

"The Starlight Ride," Jasmine and May told her.

Corey sighed. "I can't wait. Tell me more about it," she pleaded.

"Well, it takes place on Christmas Eve night," May began, "and all the riders from Pine Hollow leave from the stable and take a trail ride through the woods."

"We end up in the middle of town, singing holiday songs," Jasmine added. "Everything is decorated with red and green and there are lights and horses and ponies. It's so much fun!"

"Anything to do with Christmas is fun," May reminded her.

"And anything that has to do with both po-nies *and* Christmas is double-fun," Corey pointed out.

Her friends weren't about to argue with that! Ponies were what the three girls liked the best. Each of them had her own pony that lived in a stable in her backyard. And they all took riding lessons at Pine Hollow Stables and belonged to

Jasmine's Christmas Ride

a Pony Club called Horse Wise. Whenever the girls got together, their favorite subject was ponies. In fact, they were so pony crazy, they'd decided to call themselves the Pony Tails. It wasn't exactly a club. It was best friends. That was even better than a club.

"Now I think we're supposed to circle right," Corey called out. Jasmine and May followed her. Jasmine tried hard to keep exactly one pony length between her pony, Outlaw, and Corey's pony, Samurai. That was what Max, their riding instructor and Pony Club leader, had told them to do. But Outlaw wanted to catch up with Samurai. Jasmine held him back.

Jasmine's pony was named Outlaw because he had a white face that looked like an outlaw's mask. Jasmine loved him more than she could say—even when he acted up, which happened a lot. Outlaw knew how to hold his breath so that Jasmine couldn't tighten the girth on his saddle. He knew how to hold his mouth closed to make it hard to put the bit behind his teeth. He knew just which pockets to sniff to find carrots and apples.

He usually did what Jasmine asked him to do when she was riding him, but sometimes he got other ideas in his head. Like deciding on his own that he wanted to go back to his stall.

Pony Tails

One thing was for sure—his personality was very different from Jasmine's. But that was true of all three ponies; they were nothing like their owners.

May's pony was named Macaroni. He was yellow, the color of May's favorite food, macaroni and cheese. Macaroni was a very sweet pony. He had the gentlest and politest disposition of all the ponies. He almost never gave May any trouble. That was different from May, who sometimes liked to make trouble!

Corey's pony, Samurai, was named for the curved blaze on his face, which was shaped like a sword blade. Sometimes Samurai was a very nervous pony. When he'd first moved to Corey's new house—and his new stable—the girls had needed to show him every inch of the place before he felt comfortable. And then, one time not too long ago, he had run away and hadn't come back for a week. With such an unpredictable pony, it was lucky that Corey was a calm person. She was very good at fixing things and solving problems—especially the ones her pony caused!

As the three girls and three ponies circled the ring, Jasmine was concentrating very hard. The Starlight Ride wasn't the only exciting thing coming up for the Pony Tails. In just a

Jasmine's Christmas Ride

few weeks their Pony Club was going to do a drill team demonstration. The drill team was a little bit like a marching band on horseback, only the riders didn't have to play instruments. They had to make sure their horses walked properly in a procession. The Pony Club was performing with another club called Cross County.

A lot of people would be coming to the demonstration, and they would actually be paying to watch the Pony Clubbers ride! It was to raise money for CARL, the County Animal Rescue League, which helped animals in trouble.

Jasmine wanted to raise a lot of money for CARL and perform well in the drill. As she practiced, she kept her eyes straight ahead. Her back was straight. Her legs were in perfect position. Her heels were down, her toes pointed in. She was balanced in the saddle. She held her hands just the way Max had taught her, and she used the reins and her legs to keep Outlaw going at a steady pace. It took him a couple of strides, but once he knew what she wanted him to do, he did it. She was pleased.

"And now to the left!" said Corey.

Jasmine and Outlaw circled to the left. May and Macaroni followed them.

While Corey and Jasmine concentrated on

the drill, May was still thinking about the Starlight Ride. She was distracted and let Macaroni speed up. In a drill team all the horses were supposed to move at exactly the same speed. They had to keep the same distance between them.

"May!" Jasmine cried. May reined Macaroni in. He slowed down.

"I think I'm ready for a rest," May decided. "But that doesn't mean you guys have to stop." She rode Macaroni over to the side of the ring and sat comfortably in the saddle. Jasmine and Corey were much more interested in the drill work than she was. Right now she'd rather watch from the sidelines than practice. That way she could keep daydreaming about the Starlight Ride and how wonderful it would be!

2 Drill Practice

"Why don't you go first this time?" Corey suggested as May and Macaroni rode off.

"Me?" Jasmine said.

"Sure. You can do it," Corey said.

Jasmine patted Outlaw and told him it was time to get back to work. His ears flicked eagerly. He swished his tail. He was ready.

Jasmine nudged him and they began the exercise. They had to ride a long and complicated pattern. She remembered when to turn and when to change gaits. Once she forgot she was supposed to make a circle to the left. She went to the right. Corey reminded her, so they reversed their direction and finished the circle correctly.

May clapped for her friends when they finished the exercise. "You're both so good at this!" she said. "Maybe Max will ask both of you to lead the whole drill team!"

Jasmine didn't think Max would ever ask her, but it was nice of May to say so.

"Hey, didn't Max say something about a small group of riders doing a special show?" May asked.

"He sure did," said Corey. "He's going to pick the best riders."

"That means you'll both be on it," May said.

"No way," said Jasmine.

"Just wait and see," said May.

The ponies were tired by then; it was time to untack and groom them. The girls liked to do that together so that they could talk as they worked. They each cross-tied their ponies in the Grovers' stable.

The Grovers' stable was much bigger than either Corey's or Jasmine's. That was because May's father was a horse trainer. The Grovers owned three horses and a pony, and Mr. Grover's student horses usually stayed there during their training period. Their stable had room for eight horses. Corey's stable had room for two ponies. Jasmine's stable was more like a shed and had been built just for Outlaw.

As Corey rolled up her sleeves, Jasmine no-

Jasmine's Christmas Ride

ticed that she was wearing a colorful bead bracelet with her name woven into it.

"Oh, that's pretty!" Jasmine said.

May looked at it, too. She agreed with Jasmine. "It's got a sword on it. That's for Samurai, isn't it?" she said.

"Of course. That way Samurai is always with me." Corey smiled.

"Neat," said May.

"Thanks," said Corey. "I made it myself."

"Well, you did a good job," said Jasmine, wishing she had such a nice way to have Outlaw with her all the time.

Then she picked up her currycomb and dandy brush and set to work. Some people didn't enjoy all the work that went with owning a pony, but Jasmine and her friends liked everything that had to do with ponies—and that included the hard parts.

Jasmine looked out the window of the stable as she worked. There was no sign of snow now. Maybe she'd been wrong earlier in the day.

Still, she told herself, it might not be snowing yet, but Christmas was almost here. She felt a shiver of excitement. Christmas meant trees, presents, songs, cookies, parties, the Starlight Ride. And maybe snow.

3 Tryouts

"I've decided to pick a small group—just six of you—to perform a mini-demonstration. That will come right after the regular drill team demonstration."

Jasmine, Corey, and May were sitting next to one another on the floor of Max's office at Pine Hollow. They were having a Pony Club meeting before the regular Tuesday class. Max had just announced that he was going to pick three pairs of riders to represent Pine Hollow in the special show.

"But first we're going to have our regular class," Max went on. "Then any riders who want to try out for the special demonstration should be prepared to stay a little later. Okay, now, class will begin in fifteen minutes!"

Jasmine's Christmas Ride

That didn't give the riders much time. They had to hurry to tack up their ponies.

The Pony Tails didn't have even a minute to talk about Max's announcement before class. Nor did they when class began. Max kept them too busy.

The riders were working on what Max called manners. That meant being sure the pony or horse was well trained and polite. A pony with manners always stood still when the rider was mounting. He followed obediently on a lead rope. He didn't fight with other ponies. These were important things, but they didn't have much to do with drill skills. Jasmine wished Max had them practicing starts, stops, turns, and gait changes instead. She was afraid she'd forget everything she knew before the tryouts!

At last the class was over. Tryouts would begin in fifteen minutes.

Jasmine and Corey waited by the side of the ring. May had decided not to try out for the small team.

"You look so nervous!" May told Jasmine.

"I am nervous," Jasmine told her.

"You don't have anything to be nervous about. You two will definitely make it," May replied.

Jasmine hoped her friend was right.

Max stood in the middle of the ring and asked who was trying out. Twelve riders raised their hands. Jasmine looked at the twelve hands, and one thought came into her mind:

Only half of us will make it.

"Okay, mount up," said Max. And the try-outs began. Max had them ride in circles, he had them turn corners, and he had them change gaits. He paired them up, then split them to singles. He made two lines cross at an X in the middle of the ring, and he made pairs split to make opposite circles and meet together again. He took a lot of notes.

Then he asked each rider to follow a pattern he showed them. It wasn't easy for any of them.

Carole Hanson, one of the best older riders in Horse Wise, did a pretty good job of it. So did her friend Stevie Lake. Adam Levine got all messed up and forgot which way he was supposed to go. Betsy Cavanaugh remembered everything she was supposed to do, but she didn't do most of it very well. Her circles were too small, and her turns were more like bends. Jasmine didn't think Betsy would be invited into the small group.

Then it was Corey's turn. Jasmine was proud of her! Corey did everything right. She didn't

Jasmine's Christmas Ride

forget anything. Her corners were sharp; her circles were smooth.

"Slow down, Corey," Max said once. Corey and Sam slowed down immediately.

"Nice, but keep it even," Max added.

Corey nodded and then tried to keep her pace even. And when Corey was done, Max said, "Good." Then he said, "Jasmine?"

It was her turn. Jasmine tried to smile, but she was too nervous. She could see Max. He was making a note on his clipboard. Then she could see eleven other riders. They were all good. In fact, she thought they were all better than she was. For a moment Jasmine thought everybody in the world was better than she was. Then she remembered Betsy's mistakes. Maybe she'd be better than Betsy Cavanaugh. Maybe.

"Okay, go," Max said. "Remember, keep an even pace."

Jasmine went. She kept an even pace. That was one thing she and Outlaw were really good at. She imagined that there was a pony in front of her, and as she rode through the exercise she always kept Outlaw exactly one pony length behind the imaginary pony. She smiled to herself, thinking how nice it was to have a perfectly behaved pony in front of her to fol-

Jasmine's Christmas Ride

low. Unfortunately, that imaginary pony didn't have a very good memory, because he turned the wrong way a few times.

"No, no, Jasmine. Go left there!" said Max.

Jasmine went to the left, but then she couldn't remember what came next. When she hesitated, Max helped her again.

"Circle, Jasmine. To the right," said Max.

Jasmine circled to the right. Finally it was over.

"Nice job of keeping a steady pace," said Max. "That's not easy to do."

"Thanks," said Jasmine.

When the last rider had tried out and Max had made the last note, he gathered everyone together.

"I'll be calling the team later this week," he said, "but whether you made it or not, thank you all. You worked hard. I can't ask for anything more."

Corey and Jasmine ran their stirrups up and loosened their ponies' girths.

"You were both great," said May. "You'll both be on the team."

Jasmine wasn't so sure. She crossed her fingers for good luck.

4 The Call

Corey chewed on the end of her pencil. It tasted awful, and it didn't help her think. She was supposed to be writing a story about rain forests. It was her last assignment before Christmas vacation started. She didn't want to write about rain forests. She wanted to think about ponies. She wanted the phone to ring, too.

Corey's parents were divorced. She spent half of her time at her father's apartment. She loved being with her father. He had a nice apartment, and they always did their schoolwork together. Her father taught French and Spanish at Willow Creek High School. The only thing she didn't like about being with her father was that she couldn't bring Samurai with

Jasmine's Christmas Ride

The phone rang. Corey jumped. Her father answered it. Somebody wanted to sell him life insurance. He didn't want to buy it. He hung up the phone and returned to his desk.

Corey picked up her pencil again. "Once there was a parrot who lived in a rain forest," she wrote. "He liked to be with the other parrots. They would all fly together in formation, like a marching band." No they wouldn't, Corey said to herself. She knew parrots didn't do anything like that. But ponies did. She sighed. She tore up the paper to start fresh.

The phone rang again. Corey jumped again. Her father answered it.

"Corey, it's for you," he said. "It's Max."

She gulped and reached for the phone. "Hello?"

"Congratulations," Max said to her. Corey hardly heard anything he said after that. He'd chosen her for the small drill team! She'd done it! She was grinning so hard that her cheeks hurt. Luckily, she did hear Max say she'd have to work very hard over vacation. They would start with a practice the next day, right after school. Could she get Samurai to Pine Hollow then?

"I'll ask if Mr. Grover can bring him," she said.

"He can come over anytime tomorrow," said Max. "And then I'll see you by four o'clock. Right?"

"You bet!" she said. Then she said good-bye and hung up the phone.

For a second she didn't move. She just felt. And the feeling was wonderful. She'd known she wanted to make the team, but she hadn't known how much until it happened. She couldn't remember ever feeling better than she did right then.

"Honey?" her father said.

"I made the team!" she said breathlessly. Then she yelled. "Yahoooooo!"

Her father hugged her and congratulated her and then hugged her again.

"And what about your friend Jasmine? Did she make it, too?" he asked.

Corey had been so excited she'd forgotten to ask Max about Jasmine. But what was there to ask? Jasmine had been in Horse Wise much longer than Corey had been. She'd been riding longer than Corey. Of course Jasmine had been chosen. Corey punched in the digits of Jasmine's number, but the line was busy. She quickly called May.

May was thrilled for her. "I knew you would

do it, I just knew it!" she said. "I'm so excited for you both!"

Then Corey talked with Mr. Grover. On school days the girls didn't usually bring their own ponies to Pine Hollow. It was a lot of work to transport them there for a short class, especially when all the work had to be done by Mr. Grover, who had a horse trailer. But Mr. Grover always brought the horses over to Pine Hollow on Saturdays and special occasions.

Corey asked May's father to help her take Samurai over to Pine Hollow after school the next day.

"I can't do it in the afternoon," he said. "But I can in the morning. Why don't I just drop him off for you there so he'll be waiting for you? You can go to Pine Hollow straight from school."

"Are you sure that's not too much trouble?" Corey asked.

"I'm glad to do it for you," replied Mr. Grover.

"Thanks," Corey said. She loved Mr. Grover. He was so nice to the Pony Tails.

As soon as she got off the phone with Mr. Grover, Corey tried Jasmine again. Her line was still busy.

She's probably talking to May about the drill team, Corey thought. Or asking Mr. Grover to bring Outlaw over, too.

Corey went back to her homework. By the time she thought of calling her friend again, it was too late. Oh well, Corey told herself. I'll see Jasmine at school tomorrow. We can celebrate together there.

*   *   *

"Hello, Jasmine, this is Max."

Jasmine gripped the phone tightly. She'd been waiting for this call.

"I'm really impressed with the progress you've been making this year," Max began. "Your hard work is paying off. I wish I could choose everyone for the team, but . . ."

Max didn't have to finish his sentence.

Jasmine knew what he was about to say. She swallowed hard. It felt as if there were a huge hole in the middle of her stomach and nothing would ever fill it. Max hadn't chosen her. She hadn't made the small drill team.

"What about Corey?" Jasmine finally said. "Is she going to be on it?"

"Yes. Corey will be on it, and so will Jackie Rogers. They'll be the two youngest riders," said Max. "I hope you understand. . . ."

Jasmine's Christmas Ride

"Sure," Jasmine mumbled. Then she hung up.

She understood all right. It was very clear. Max was saying she wasn't as good as the other riders—including her best friend Corey.

5 First Practice

The next day Corey didn't ride the bus with May and Jasmine because she was at her father's apartment. And she didn't see them at school, either. The whole schedule had been changed around because it was the last day before vacation.

At the end of the day, Corey's class had a holiday party in their classroom. Their teacher served juice and gingerbread cookies. Then everyone was supposed to make an ornament for the tree in the center of town.

Corey cut a star out of cardboard and wrapped it in aluminum foil. It wasn't much of an ornament, but it would have to do. She was too excited about the drill team practice to think about anything else—even Christmas ornaments.

The second the bell sounded, Corey put on her coat. Her book bag was already packed. She was out the door before the bell stopped ringing.

Corey stood on the school steps waiting for Jasmine and May. She wanted to talk to Jasmine about the drill team practice and walk to Pine Hollow with her. As she waited, the cold wind whipped around her. But after ten minutes there was still no sign of Jasmine or May.

Today the whole school day had been different, Corey thought. Maybe their teachers had let them out early.

Finally she shrugged and hurried down the steps.

Pine Hollow Stable was just a short walk from Willow Creek Elementary School. But waiting for Jasmine and May had made Corey late. By the time she got to the stable, riders were already warming up their horses in the indoor ring. Corey glanced over at them, but she didn't see Jasmine. She must be changing her clothes, Corey thought. She hurried to the locker area. It was empty.

She shoved her books into her cubby and quickly changed into her riding clothes. There wasn't a minute to spare. She wanted to catch up with Jasmine in the stable where they could tack up their ponies together.

Samurai was waiting for her. Max had put him in an empty stall near Pine Hollow's ponies. His tack was there, too. As usual, Mr. Grover had kept his promise. Corey would have to thank him later.

Corey looked around for Jasmine and Outlaw. But they weren't in the stable, either.

Sam was as eager to get going as Corey was. He behaved perfectly while she gave him a quick brushing and then put on his saddle and bridle. Red O'Malley, Max's assistant, gave Corey a hand tightening the girth. He held Samurai while she mounted him, then handed her the reins.

"Don't forget the good-luck horseshoe!" he reminded her.

"I won't," she promised.

Pine Hollow had a horseshoe nailed to the wall by the door that led to the outside ring. Every rider was supposed to touch it before heading out. It was one of Pine Hollow's many traditions. No rider who had touched the shoe

had ever gotten seriously hurt in a riding accident.

Corey gave it a quick touch and then turned Samurai around to enter the indoor ring, where the practice would take place. Max was there. He looked at his watch and then nodded a greeting. It was exactly four o'clock. Corey had made it on time—just barely.

She sighed with relief, settled into her saddle, and began her warm-up circles around the ring. She looked at the other riders doing the same thing.

But something was wrong. Jasmine wasn't there.

Uh-oh, Corey thought. Maybe Jasmine's still waiting for me at school. Or worse—Corey swallowed—maybe something has happened to her.

But Max didn't seem to notice Jasmine's absence.

"All right," he called. "Now that we're all here, come on over and let me tell you what our program will be."

Now that we're all here. Max's words rang in Corey's ears. They weren't all there. Jasmine was still missing.

Jasmine's Christmas Ride

Quickly Corey counted the other riders. There were five of them. Corey made six.

Then, for the first time, Corey understood. Jasmine wasn't in the small group.

Corey had been chosen and Jasmine hadn't!

6 Christmas Cookies

"Can you find the sugar?" May asked Jasmine.

Jasmine looked around the Grovers' kitchen. It wasn't easy to find anything. A fine white dust covered almost everything. That had happened when May dropped an entire bin of flour on the floor. May wasn't exactly the neatest baker in the world.

Jasmine opened one of the bins on the counter. Coffee. The next was filled with tea. The last was sugar. She handed it to May.

May began measuring two cups of sugar to add to the bowl in front of her. Jasmine added the vanilla and the eggs.

The two of them were at May's house making Christmas cookies. When May had invited Jasmine over, Jasmine had hoped baking cook-

Jasmine's Christmas Ride

ies would keep her from thinking about Max's phone call last night.

And she knew May was hoping the same thing.

Jasmine handed May a wooden spoon and then went to find the baking soda.

"I think it's over the stove," May said. "Or else it's in the cabinet by the refrigerator, or maybe—"

"I'll find it," Jasmine said. She did, too. She only had to look in five cabinets, and then there it was.

The kitchen door swung open. It was Mrs. Grover. One glance around the kitchen and her face turned as pale as the coat of flour that covered the floor.

"May—" she began.

"No problem, Mom," May said brightly. "Jasmine and I have read the recipe very carefully. You're going to *love* our cookies!"

Mrs. Grover didn't look at all convinced. Jasmine thought it wasn't the cookies she was worried about. It was the mess in the kitchen.

"You've got to—" Mrs. Grover said.

"I know, Mom. You want us to remember to use mitts when we take the cookies out of the oven. Don't worry. We won't burn our fingers."

Jasmine's Christmas Ride

"Don't you—" Mrs. Grover started again.

"And we promise not to test the cookies before they're cool. We don't want to burn our tongues, either."

"I hope—" Mrs. Grover tried to say.

"We won't eat them all. I promise. There'll be enough for everybody."

"The mess!" Mrs. Grover said finally.

"I'll help clean up," Jasmine promised.

Mrs. Grover nodded weakly, then left the room.

"See? She trusts us!" May said brightly.

Jasmine wasn't sure May was right about that. But May sounded so positive, it was hard to disagree.

May added the baking soda to the batter and chatted about what they could bake for the rest of the afternoon. "First we'll finish these sugar cookies, and then I want to do some chocolate chips and some peanut butter cookies. But my very favorites are the almond ones, so we can do them after the peanut butter—or should we do them before?"

Jasmine glanced around the messy kitchen. "I think I'd better keep track of which cookies we're baking," she said. She went to her book bag and took out her loose-leaf binder.

Pony Tails

"You're so organized," May sighed. "I wish I were as good at that as you are."

Jasmine shrugged. Who cared about being organized? It would be much better to be able to ride as well as Corey.

She flipped open her notebook and reached for a pencil in the pocket of her book bag.

"Wow," May went on. "You actually know where your pencils are, too!"

Jasmine looked up at her friend. "You can stop trying to make me feel good, May," she said. "It's not working."

"I'm . . . I . . . but don't you think . . ." May didn't know what to say.

"Look, May," Jasmine cut in, "you don't have to say anything. The truth is, Corey did better than I did at the tryouts. That's why I didn't get picked." Jasmine's eyes started to fill with tears. She gulped and stopped talking.

"I'm not on the small drill team either," May said softly.

"You didn't try out," Jasmine reminded her. "If you had, you'd probably be on it. You're definitely better than I am, too."

"Maybe I am—at some things," said May. "But not everything. Nobody's good at everything."

May stuck the spoon in the cookie dough.

Jasmine's Christmas Ride

But it was stiff and hard to mix. Jasmine took the spoon and tried it for a while.

"See, you're better at cookie baking than I am," May pointed out. "And you found the baking soda when I had no idea where it was."

"May!" Jasmine cried. "Cut it out. You're making me feel worse!"

May sighed. She wanted to make Jasmine feel better. But there wasn't anything she could say that would change the situation. Corey was on the team. Jasmine wasn't.

May stopped trying to cheer up Jasmine for a while. They just worked on the cookies.

A half hour later, three batches of sugar cookies were cooling on the counter. Jasmine's half was neatly decorated. The other half was a mess. Sprinkles were scattered everywhere, and May's fingerprints were visible in the middle of several of the cookies.

Jasmine giggled.

"Who cares?" May said. "They taste good, don't they?"

Jasmine bit into one and nodded.

It was time to start the next batch of dough. Jasmine consulted her list.

"Chocolate chips next," she said, and then she closed the notebook.

"Hey, that's nice," said May.

"What's nice?" asked Jasmine.

"Your notebook," said May. "Can I see it?"

"Sure." Jasmine had covered her entire loose-leaf notebook with pictures of ponies and horses.

"I cut them from horse show programs and the Pony Club magazine," she explained. "I pasted them onto the notebook and covered it with clear plastic paper. It looks cool, doesn't it?"

Without thinking, May blurted out, "See, you're organized and you're artistic and"—she picked up one of Jasmine's cookies and stared at it—"you're a much better cookie decorator than I am."

Jasmine shrugged. Then she looked down at the counter and began to work on the chocolate chips.

May knew immediately she'd said the wrong thing again. Jasmine wanted to hear she was good at riding—not that she was good at baking or art or anything else.

The two girls worked quietly for the next hour.

After the last sheet of peanut butter cookies went into the oven, Jasmine announced that it was time for her to go home.

"Already?" said May.

Jasmine's Christmas Ride

"My mother's expecting me," Jasmine told her. She picked up her books and her jacket and left by the kitchen door before May could even give her a box of cookies.

May watched her friend go, then dropped down on a stool. Mrs. James wasn't expecting Jasmine, and May knew it. Jasmine had just wanted to go home.

"Oh well," May mumbled. Her plan for today hadn't worked out, but May would try to cheer up Jasmine again tomorrow.

In the meantime, she had another project—cleaning up the kitchen. Every inch of the room was covered with empty bowls, flour, sugar, eggshells, and globs of butter. Sugar sprinkles, chopped nuts, and frosting were scattered everywhere.

So far, trying to make Jasmine feel better was hard work!

7 Saturday at Pine Hollow

The next morning May sat between her two friends on the backseat of her father's van. No one said a word.

May looked at Corey. She was staring out the window. May looked at Jasmine. She was staring at her hands. Today even the three ponies in the trailer were noisier than the three Pony Tails in the van.

It wasn't easy when your two best friends couldn't say the things they wanted to say. May couldn't say those things for them, either. If she'd been able to, she would have told Corey that Jasmine wanted to be on the small drill team. And she would have told Jasmine that Corey wished she were on the team.

May wanted to say these things, but she

Jasmine's Christmas Ride

knew that her friends would have to find ways to say them to one another.

May knew she just had to be patient. But being patient was not what May did best.

Mr. Grover drove the van into Pine Hollow. Max greeted them, and Mr. Grover helped the girls get their ponies tacked up. It was unusual for Horse Wise to have two mounted meetings in a row, but there was still a lot of work to do on the drill exercise.

With some help from Red O'Malley, the head stable hand at Pine Hollow, Corey got Sam's tack on quickly. She touched the good-luck horseshoe and began circling the indoor ring at a walk. It was only yesterday that she'd been there for her small group practice. Sam glanced back at her as if he were surprised about being in the ring again today.

Corey patted his neck, lost in her thoughts. If only Jasmine were part of the small group, too! Sometimes Corey still felt like the new kid at Pine Hollow. She'd moved to Willow Creek pretty recently and had just joined Horse Wise. She felt funny being picked for the drill team when Jasmine hadn't been. Especially since Jasmine was just as good a rider as Corey.

Corey felt tears welling up in her eyes.

Pony Tails

*　　　*　　　*

Inside the area where the horses' stalls were, Jasmine took longer than her friends to get Outlaw tacked up. He was trying to play a trick on her. Every time she went to tighten up his girth, he filled his chest with air. Normally this made her laugh. Today she wasn't in a laughing mood. She glared at her pony.

"I see what you're doing," she said. Outlaw blinked as if he were bored. "You're not fooling me."

All Jasmine had to do was wait. The pony couldn't hold his breath forever. She patted his neck and then began waiting.

As she held the girth in her hand and stared at his belly, she tried to picture yesterday's practice. Had Corey been in the lead? She probably had been because Max liked to pair the riders by size, and Corey was one of the smallest.

Had she done well? Definitely, Jasmine thought. Corey did well at everything.

Was there music with the drill exercise? Max was probably using marching music. Jasmine could almost hear the wonderful beat of horses' hooves, marching in time, moving in perfect unison through a precision exercise.

Pony Tails

I'd make a mistake, Jasmine thought. I'd turn left instead of right, or mess up the trot. No wonder Max didn't pick me. And Corey probably never wants to ride with me again!

Suddenly Outlaw let out his breath. Before he could take in another couple of gallons of air, Jasmine pulled the leather of his girth two holes tighter.

"Gotcha," she said. The job was done.

*   *   *

When everybody was in the ring, Max had them all line up.

"We've been working so hard on the drill that I haven't even had time to remind you about something else that comes up even before that," he said.

"Oh, the Starlight Ride!" Jasmine blurted out.

"Thank you, Jasmine," said Max. He sounded a little sarcastic, but his blue eyes were twinkling. "Yes, it's the Starlight Ride."

Max looked at Corey. "Those of you who have been here for a while know about this tradition, but we do have some new riders who don't know."

"You're going to love it!" May whispered to Corey.

Jasmine's Christmas Ride

"Thank you, May," said Max. "You Pony Tails are being very helpful today," he teased.

As Jasmine listened to Max talking about the Starlight Ride, her thoughts about Corey and the drill team drifted away. Christmas Eve at Pine Hollow was the most magical time of the year. The path through the woods would be decorated with lights, and the riders would proceed in a straight line to the center of the town, where a crowd would be gathered. Last year May and Jasmine had had a wonderful time. This year . . . Jasmine looked at Corey. She had been hoping that the three of them would have an even better time. But—

"This year I've asked Stevie Lake to lead the ride," Max cut into Jasmine's thoughts.

Jasmine knew it was a big honor to be in the lead. Max always chose a young rider who showed excellent progress. It had to be someone who could ride well but also someone who'd worked hard through the year. And because almost everyone in Willow Creek watched, it had to be someone Max completely trusted to do a good job.

As everyone looked around for Stevie, Max explained, "Stevie isn't here now. She and her friends are visiting a dude ranch until Wednesday. They'll be back in time for the ride, though. I want you all here at six o'clock on Wednesday evening."

"What time does the ride start?" asked Corey.

"Seven," said Max. "But we'll tack up and warm up and have inspection before we leave. Wear warm clothes over proper riding attire. I don't want to see a speck of mud on anybody's saddle or a scruffy coat on anybody's horse or pony. Remember, the whole town of Willow Creek will be watching us!"

Jasmine was thinking so hard about Christmas and the Starlight Ride, she didn't hear Max tell everyone to begin a trot. Then Outlaw began trotting. At least he was listening!

Once the ponies and horses were all warmed up, Max started working on the big drill exercise. Max worked the riders hard. There was no time to think about the Starlight Ride or anything else.

"To the right, Jackie!" Max yelled when Jackie Rogers turned the wrong way.

"Hey, Amie, not so fast!" he called out when Amie Connor's pony started catching up to the pony in front of her.

"Veronica! Pay attention!" he said to Veronica diAngelo.

Jasmine's Christmas Ride

Jasmine was glad that Max didn't yell at her.

Corey was relieved not to hear her own name called out.

May was glad that all the Pony Tails seemed to be doing a good job.

Finally, at the end of the Horse Wise meeting, Max had the riders line up one more time.

"You've done a lot of good work," he said. "You're almost ready to perform with Cross County. Now I'm going to dismiss everybody except the six riders in the small group. We'll have one more mounted meeting next Saturday, and then we'll be at Cross County the following Saturday. Next week is our dress rehearsal. Are we ready?"

"Yes *sir!*" May said. She saluted him. Some of the riders laughed.

Max grinned. "Okay, then Horse Wise dis-*missed!*"

May and Jasmine rode Macaroni and Outlaw back into the stall area, where they would untack and groom their ponies.

Jasmine tried not to look at or listen to Max as he went on talking to the group that was left behind.

But she couldn't help it.

Pony Tails

"Now, what were we working on when we stopped yesterday?" Max asked the small group.

Corey's hand went up.

Jasmine sighed. If only she were with them!

8 Waiting for Corey

Jasmine removed Outlaw's saddle and bridle and cross-tied him so that she could groom him while they waited for Mr. Grover. Since Mr. Grover was going to take all their ponies home at once, he wasn't coming until after Corey's practice.

Outlaw stood absolutely still while Jasmine groomed him. As she worked, she could still hear Max talking to the small group.

"All together now! . . . Better . . . Come on, catch up there . . . No! Not that way! Turn left! Heels down. Look where you're going! Sit into the saddle! Tell your pony what you want him to do, don't just let him follow! . . . Use your crop if you need to. Your aids! Your aids! That's how you tell your pony what to do! . . .

Okay, let's begin again! And do it right this time. You know what you're supposed to do."

Max was working the riders very hard. He was being fussier with the small group than he had been with the whole of Horse Wise. Jasmine thought again about what it would be like to be there. Would she remember to turn the right way? Could she keep her heels down? Would she use her crop correctly? Max sometimes had to remind her about those things in class. It would be even harder to be reminded in a small group.

"Corey!" Max said sharply. Then he said something else. Jasmine couldn't hear what it was, but he didn't sound happy. She cringed for Corey.

Jasmine tried to think about something else. She thought about Christmas instead. It was only a few days away and she still had a lot to do—like make presents for May and Corey. Then there was the Starlight Ride. Maybe, just maybe, it *would* snow this year. That would make it just about perfect.

But the way things are going this year, Jasmine thought a second later, the Starlight Ride will get rained out. And then both May and

Jasmine's Christmas Ride

Corey are going to hate the presents I'm making for them, and . . .

Within a very few minutes, Jasmine had convinced herself that this was going to be the worst Christmas ever—worse even than the year her grandmother gave her the blue dress with purple flowers and made her wear it all Christmas day.

*　　*　　*

From the other side of the stable, May could just barely see Jasmine over the heads of Barq and Nero. Part of her was sorry to be so far from both of her friends. Another part of her was very glad. It wasn't easy being in the middle. It seemed that every time she said something to comfort Jasmine, it was the wrong thing. And everytime she brought up the small drill team to Corey, Corey just changed the subject.

May took off Macaroni's saddle and put it on a sawhorse. She reached into her pony's grooming bucket. She always started by picking Macaroni's hooves. He sometimes fussed when she did that, so she liked to get it over with first.

She looked for her hoof pick. She didn't see

it. She dumped the entire contents of her grooming bucket on the ground. All her other grooming tools were there, plus two pencils and part of last week's sandwich, but no hoof pick.

May tossed the sandwich crusts into the garbage and went to ask Mrs. Reg if she could borrow a hoof pick. May was pretty sure Mrs. Reg would be willing to lend her one.

Mrs. Reg was Max's mother and the manager of the stables. She had a way of telling long stories to the young riders at the most unexpected times. Her stories were always about horses and were always interesting. It just wasn't always clear *why* she was telling them. Still, May needed a hoof pick, so she had to take a chance. She went into Mrs. Reg's office.

Mrs. Reg was at her desk, sorting out Christmas decorations. A mess of tinsel garland was spread across the floor. Mrs. Reg was trying to untangle it. She seemed glad to have an interruption.

"Sure," she said in answer to May's request. She dropped the tinsel on the floor and went to her desk drawer. She took out a hoof pick and looked at it before handing it to May.

"This is a well-designed tool," said Mrs. Reg.

Pony Tails

Uh-oh, May thought. Is this the beginning of a story?

But it wasn't.

"It's good for only one thing," Mrs. Reg went on.

"Yes it is," said May. She didn't think Mrs. Reg would want to know about the time Corey used a hoof pick to fix one of Jasmine's dolls.

"It's good only for picking hooves. It won't do at all to bang in a nail or open a can. There are much better tools for that," said Mrs. Reg.

"Definitely," May agreed. Mrs. Reg handed her the hoof pick.

A few minutes later May returned the hoof pick to Mrs. Reg's office. Mrs. Reg wasn't there; neither was the tinsel garland. May was a little relieved Mrs. Reg was gone. She put the hoof pick on her desk. She'd been worried she might hear more about how wonderful a hoof pick is. Sometimes, May thought, Mrs. Reg doesn't make much sense.

By the time May had finished grooming Macaroni, her father had arrived. She and Jasmine loaded Macaroni and Outlaw into the trailer. Then Corey's practice was over. She led Samurai out to the driveway where the van was parked.

Jasmine loosened Sam's girth. May led him

up the ramp of the trailer. Corey put Sam's grooming bucket in the storage area and climbed into the car. May and Jasmine climbed in with her. Mr. Grover started the engine and pulled out onto the road.

"Say, if you girls want to practice some more this afternoon, you can use our ring," said Mr. Grover. "Max told me that there's a lot of work yet to do on the drill exercise."

"No thanks."

"No thanks."

"No thanks."

All three girls spoke at almost the same second. Usually when the Pony Tails did that—said the same thing at the same time—they'd give one another high and low fives and then say "Jake." This time, though, they didn't even look at each other. They just made excuses.

"I think Macaroni's a little tired," said May.

"I promised my mother I'd help her with some of the pets she's boarding now," said Corey. "I said I'd feed them."

"I have to wash my hair," said Jasmine.

Then each member of the Pony Tails hurried away to her own house.

9 The Pony Tails Have Secrets

"Here you go, Outlaw." Jasmine gave her pony a fresh bucket of water and hurried back to her house. She ran her fingers through her hair. It didn't need to be washed at all. She had something much more important to do that she couldn't tell Corey and May about. It was a secret.

She walked through the living room and looked at the Christmas cards her mother had put on display. They were so festive that just looking at them made her feel a little better. She hummed "Jingle Bells" as she ran upstairs.

In her room she changed out of her riding clothes and into her jeans and a big T-shirt so that she wouldn't mess up her good clothes while she worked. She took out her materials:

Jasmine's Christmas Ride

scissors, glue, magazines, posters, and all the pictures she'd already found. She also had two plain loose-leaf binders. They weren't going to be plain for long!

This was her Christmas present for May and for Corey. She knew May would love hers. She wasn't so sure about Corey. They had said so little to each other lately, Jasmine wasn't sure about a lot of things that had to do with her friend.

The big question was, which pictures should go on each notebook? Samurai was a dark-colored pony. She could find a lot of pictures of dark ponies and cover Corey's binder with them, but then she might have trouble with May's. Macaroni's coat was light. Jasmine didn't have very many pictures of macaroni-colored ponies.

But she did have one big picture of a yellow pony that looked a lot like Macaroni. And she did have one big picture of a pony with a curved blaze almost like Samurai's. That was the answer, then. She'd put the pony that looked most like Macaroni on the middle of May's binder. The one that looked like Sam would go on Corey's binder. Then she'd mix up all the other pictures.

Jasmine smiled. For the first time since

Pony Tails

Thursday, she felt really happy. Her friends were going to *love* their Christmas presents. Even Corey. Maybe *especially* Corey.

*   *   *

Next door Corey was also hard at work. She hadn't exactly been lying when she'd said she had to look after some of the animals her mother was boarding. She'd just been stretching the truth. This weekend they had only one cat staying with them. It took Corey about twenty-three seconds to fill the cat's food and water bowls. It took her another seven seconds to pat her gently. Then she hurried up to her room. There was a lot of work to do and very little time to do it. Christmas was just a few days away. She would have to spend some of each of those days at Pine Hollow practicing for the small drill team program. And then there would be the Starlight Ride. She wondered what that was going to be like. Riding at night sounded like so much fun!

On top of everything else, Corey needed time to make her friends' presents. She wanted to do something very special—especially for Jasmine. The two of them still weren't speaking very much. Corey wanted Jasmine to know how sad she was that Jasmine hadn't made the small drill team.

She rolled up her sleeves. She was wearing the beaded bracelet she'd made for herself. She remembered how her friends had admired it the week before. Now they were going to get ones just like it!

She took out the small loom she'd used to make her own bracelet, beads, thread, and a needle. She had a dish for each color of beads. She also got out her graph paper. She'd made a special pattern for each of her friends. May's bracelet would say "May" on it when it was done, but it would also have a picture of some macaroni. Jasmine's bracelet would have her name plus a mask—the kind an outlaw would wear.

She checked her chart. "First row all blue," she said. She fished seven blue beads from the blue-bead bowl and put them on the needle.

She couldn't wait to give the bracelets to her friends!

*   *   *

In the house next door May was very busy. The first part of her job was in the kitchen. She filled two boxes with cookies for her friends. It

Jasmine's Christmas Ride

didn't seem right to give Jasmine the cookies Jasmine had made herself. So May carefully chose the best ones she'd made and put them in a box for Jasmine. When she started filling Corey's box, it didn't seem right for May to give Corey the cookies Jasmine had made. So she gave her the rest of the good ones May had done. While she was working, May ate a few of the cookies Jasmine had made. That did seem fair. They were delicious, too.

When the boxes were full, she went up to her bedroom. She had more work to do there. She took out a big carton from her closet and opened it up. Inside was a large scrapbook. It was her big present for her friends and it was a present for herself, too. She'd thought it would be fun if the Pony Tails kept a scrapbook of everything they did. It would help them remember the things they were learning about ponies, but it would also help them remember the fun times they were having.

That is, if Jasmine and Corey ever started talking to each other again, May thought.

On the cover of the scrapbook, May had written "Pony Tails" in large letters. She'd made the *y* in the word *pony* from the tail of a picture of a pony. May thought it was really cute, and she was sure her friends would, too.

Pony Tails

Soon they'd have lots of pictures for the scrapbook. May's mother had promised to take instant photos of all of them at the Starlight Ride. That was only four days away, and May couldn't wait. Those pictures could go in the scrapbook on Christmas morning.

And in front of her she had pictures her father had taken of the three of them one day in their practice ring. They were all on their ponies and all smiling.

As she gazed at the pictures, May felt a little sad. Everything had seemed so simple then. Corey hadn't been in the small group. Jasmine hadn't thought she was a terrible rider. And May hadn't been in the middle. All three Pony Tails had been exactly equal.

Then May thought some more. No, that wasn't quite true. They hadn't all been equal. They had all been themselves, and each of them was very different from the others. That meant they were each good at different things, too. If only Jasmine could see it that way.

May knew that Jasmine was good at a lot of things. She was very good with cookies. She could also sew and draw well. In fact, she was much better than May or Corey at all of those things. And Jasmine was very good at taking care of Outlaw and riding him. She was a care-

Jasmine's Christmas Ride

ful, deliberate rider. She followed Max's directions and remembered them. She wasn't afraid to try new things. Jasmine *was* a good rider.

May reached for her scissors to trim one of the pictures. When she looked in her hand, though, she wasn't holding the scissors. She'd picked up her hoof pick. *This* was where she'd left it! It wouldn't do at all for trimming a picture. She stood up to search for the scissors.

While she did that, she remembered what Mrs. Reg had said earlier about the hoof pick. It was a good tool because it was designed to do one thing better than anything else. Sometimes people were a little like that—not that they were good for just one thing, but they were sometimes *better* at one thing than another.

Slowly a little smile broke out on May's face. Had Mrs. Reg been trying to tell her something after all?

10 Preparations

On Wednesday evening the three girls piled into the backseat of Mr. Grover's van. They were all in their very best riding clothes, and their ponies were in the trailer behind the van. They were on their way to Pine Hollow. It was Christmas Eve and time for the Starlight Ride.

The Pony Tails were sitting in the same seats they'd been in on Saturday: May in the middle and Corey and Jasmine far apart. They looked at one another. There was an awkward moment of silence.

Outside the car, the town of Willow Creek seemed to be dressed up for Christmas Eve, too. Houses sparkled with colored lights. Trees draped with garlands stood in front windows. A house on one side of the road had a manger

Jasmine's Christmas Ride

scene in its front yard. Across the street a bright Santa Claus was headed for a chimney. His reindeer waited impatiently on the roof.

Mr. Grover turned onto Main Street and drove past the center of town, where, later, the riders would meet up with the singers and the snacks. There, on the town green, was a traditional crèche with the newborn baby and his parents in a stable. Next to the crèche was a very tall evergreen tree. Eleven and a half months of the year, it was a plain evergreen. Tonight it was ablaze with holiday cheer.

The tree had strings of golden lights all over it that seemed to make it glow. At its top there was an angel. Her wings were open wide, welcoming and warm. And the whole tree seemed to dance with decorations, paper chains, origami animals, and aluminum-foil cutouts. They were the decorations Willow Creek's schoolchildren made every year for the tree. The Starlight Ride, and the party that followed, brought the whole town together.

It took May's breath away. She glanced at her friends on either side of her and knew they were thinking exactly what she was thinking.

"Jake," May whispered. She held up her hands for high fives.

"Jake?" Jasmine echoed softly.

Pony Tails

"But we didn't say anything," said Corey.

"Well, we were all thinking the same thing, weren't we?" asked May.

Silence followed.

Then Corey spoke up. She stared straight at Jasmine. "I was thinking about how much I love Christmas. And about how much I love being part of Pony Tails."

May held up her hands again. "Exactly."

This time her friends slapped her hands high and then low.

"Jake!" they all said together.

Jasmine glanced at Corey. "I'm sorry," she said. "I know I haven't been the nicest friend in the world." She stopped, trying to think of a way to say what she felt.

"It's okay," Corey said quickly. "I'm sorry, too. Being on the small team isn't much fun without you."

May sat between her two friends, listening to them talk. Finally! she thought. She'd tried to stay quiet while they patched things up, but suddenly she couldn't hold it in anymore.

"It's about time," she burst out. She let out a deep breath. "I was worried you two wouldn't talk to each other again until next year!"

Jasmine and Corey giggled. It was just like May to act so dramatic!

Jasmine's Christmas Ride

A few minutes later Mr. Grover pulled the van into the Pine Hollow driveway. There were three other vans there, too. A lot of young riders were going on the Starlight Ride this year.

The Pony Tails climbed out of the van and unloaded their ponies. All around them was confusion.

Adam Levine was looking for his stirrups. Jackie Rogers wanted to know if she could ride in front of Amie Connor. Three people were asking where Max was. And Max was asking where Stevie Lake was.

May looked around.

Stevie Lake was one of the Pony Tails' favorite older riders in Horse Wise. She had amazing ways of getting into trouble and even more amazing ways of getting out of it. May sometimes thought she ought to take lessons from Stevie. Tonight, however, it was hard to imagine how Stevie would get out of trouble. She was supposed to be here to lead the ride, and Max was really annoyed.

"Where *is* that girl?" he asked everybody he saw.

Nobody had seen her. May wondered if Stevie might be in the stable. She stood on tiptoes to look inside. She could see Stevie's horse, Belle. Belle was still in her stall. Belle didn't know where Stevie was, either—or if she did, she wasn't telling.

"Did you bring warm gloves?" Mrs. Reg asked the Pony Tails.

"Yes, two pairs," Jasmine said. "Mom made me bring a backup."

"Good," said Mrs. Reg. "Because Jackie's mother forgot to make her bring any. Can she borrow a pair?"

Jasmine gladly handed them over. Her mother would be happy they'd come in handy.

The Pony Tails tied their ponies up at the fence where the line of riders would assemble to start the procession. They stood and watched the confusion around them.

"Are we missing something?" May asked.

"I don't think so; what do you mean?" Corey said.

"I mean everybody but us seems to have forgotten or lost something and here we are, ready to go."

Jasmine and Corey laughed. Only May would think they might have done something wrong because they *hadn't* done anything wrong!

Max stomped over to the fence. "Did I already ask you if you've seen Stevie?"

Jasmine's Christmas Ride

"Three times," Corey replied.

"And we haven't," said Jasmine.

"Oh no," said Max.

"I can call her if you want," said May.

"Good idea," said Max. "Use the phone in Mrs. Reg's office. I'd do it myself, but I have to see if I can fix a loose shoe on Barq."

May left Macaroni with her friends and ran over to Mrs. Reg's office. She knew Stevie's phone number because they'd worked on a project together. May was worried about Stevie. She could be a little wild, and she could get into a lot of trouble. But she wasn't irresponsible. Being late to lead the Starlight Ride was irresponsible. May hoped Stevie was all right.

On the third ring Mrs. Lake answered the phone. May told her who she was and asked for Stevie.

"Oh, Stevie's not here," said Mrs. Lake. "She's at the dude ranch with her friends."

"But aren't they coming back today?" May asked.

"Well, they were *supposed* to," Mrs. Lake began, "but Mother Nature had another idea. There was a big snowstorm in the mountains out there. Their plane couldn't take off. Didn't

Max get the message? I called earlier and left a message on his machine."

May could see the blinking red light on Mrs. Reg's answering machine. "You mean Stevie won't be here for the Starlight Ride?" May asked.

"I'm afraid not," said Mrs. Lake. "We don't expect her home for at least a couple of days."

May thanked Mrs. Lake and hung up. She stood with her hand on the phone for a few minutes, thinking. A couple of days? The Starlight Ride couldn't wait that long! There were horses and ponies to ride, songs to sing, food to eat, and best of all a tree to admire. Hundreds, maybe thousands, of people would be waiting for the riders by the tree and the crèche. It was the best, most important, trail ride of the year—and the Starlight Ride didn't have a leader!

May's mind raced. She had an idea. It was a good one. Now all she had to do was convince Max. First she had to find him.

He wasn't in his office or the tack room. He wasn't in the locker area. He wasn't by the driveway.

Then she remembered. He was trying to fix a

nail in Barq's shoe. She went to Barq's stall. Max was finishing the emergency shoe repair.

"Stevie's not coming, Max," May told him.

"Not coming! How could she—" Max's face turned red.

May explained the situation before Max could explode. "She and her friends are stuck out West because of a snowstorm. Her mother called and left a message on your machine, but I guess everybody's been too busy to listen to messages."

Max nodded. Then he scratched his head thoughtfully.

"Mrs. Lake said they wouldn't be back for a couple of days," May went on. "We won't postpone the Starlight Ride, will we?"

"No, of course not," he said. He patted Barq and then handed the horse's lead rope to a rider. He stepped out of Barq's stall.

Three riders were waiting to ask Max questions. May didn't think any of the questions were as important as the one she wanted to ask him, but she knew she had to wait.

He answered the riders' questions. "Take a hat from the hat wall; tell your parents to meet us at the town center; no, you can't change horses."

Pony Tails

Those were easy questions. May's question was going to be harder. She wasn't sure exactly how to ask it.

Amie came up then and said, "Max, Mrs. Reg is looking for you."

He nodded and turned to go to his mother's office.

"Max, I wonder if—" May began.

Amie interrupted her. "Mrs. Reg says it's important."

Max started walking faster. May followed him. She tried again. "Do you think—"

"May, would you go tell all the riders to line up in order now?" Max said. "It's almost time to go. I'll be there in a minute."

"Okay, but—"

"Thanks, May," he said. Then he dashed off.

May stamped her foot. She knew Max had important things to do, but why couldn't he have waited to hear what she had to say?

When she returned to the paddock, she found that almost all the riders were ready. She climbed up onto a fence so that people could see her, and she told them he'd be there in just a minute. For now he wanted them to mount up and get in line.

Everyone was mounted and in order by the

Jasmine's Christmas Ride

time Max and his mother came out of her office.

"I've just gotten some news," he said to the group. "Stevie Lake can't be here tonight. She and Carole Hanson and Lisa Atwood are stuck out West in a snowstorm. That means our lead rider isn't here and we need a new one."

The riders looked around at one another. Leading the Starlight Ride was an important job—and an honor. Who was Max going to choose?

"I need some very special qualities in a lead rider," he told them.

May knew that. She had to bite her lip to keep from yelling out a name.

"It has to be someone we can all count on," Max explained. "It has to be someone who has good sense and can ride well. It also has to be someone who can set an even pace and stick to it so that we can all follow."

Several horses in the procession pawed the ground nervously. May held her breath as Max continued. "So, this year, I would like our leader to be . . . Jasmine James!"

Jasmine gasped with surprise. Max had chosen *her* to be the leader? She couldn't believe it.

Corey and May clapped their friend on the

back proudly. Several other riders congratulated her.

"Now, May, was there something you wanted to say to me?" Max asked.

"Uh . . . ," May began, then grinned. "I just wanted to tell you that you can read minds as well as you can ride horses!"

11 In the Lead

Jasmine looked around, afraid that if she blinked, everything would disappear. Could this be coming true? Was it real? Was she actually about to lead the Starlight Ride?

It was a crystal-clear, dark night, cool and fresh. All around her, riders and horses waited. It seemed that the world was a sea of red, green, silver, and gold holiday decorations. The Pine Hollow stable was red. Mrs. Reg had put miles of tinsel garland around each of the doors and lit them with green and gold lights. Ahead of her there was a path made by lanterns to show the way to all the riders. Most of all, it was supposed to guide Jasmine. She was in the lead.

Around her there was a hubbub of noise. Everyone was excited. Everyone was ready to go. Even Max. He walked toward her, carrying a flaming torch. It was for her.

"Here you go," he said. Jasmine took the torch from him. "Is it okay? Can you ride with it?" he asked.

Tonight, she thought, I could ride anywhere, carrying anything.

That wasn't what she said to Max, though. What she said was, "Yes. I'll be fine."

"Good luck," he told her.

But Jasmine was sure she already had it.

"Riders forward!" she cried as loudly as she could. It was her first official act as leader of the Starlight Ride. An instant later, the ride began.

She held the torch high so that everybody could see where she was going and follow her. Jasmine and Outlaw had ridden on this trail many times before. But tonight was very different, and both she and Outlaw knew it.

Outlaw's gait was a walk, but it felt more like a march. He held his head proudly and lifted each foot carefully. It was as if he knew he was in front and he wanted to show all the other ponies and horses how good he was.

For her part, Jasmine felt very special. She was doing something fun and something she was good at. She took in a deep breath of fresh night air and sighed happily. If she'd had a free hand, she might have pinched herself to be sure she wasn't dreaming!

It didn't take long for the ponies and horses to cross the fields behind Pine Hollow and reach the woods. There were a lot of trails in the woods. If it had been a dark night, even Jasmine might have gotten lost. But tonight sparkling lights lit the way. The forest seemed to shimmer with the decorations. And the sky glowed with stars. No wonder it was called the Starlight Ride, Jasmine thought. On Christmas Eve, the sky seemed almost part of the trail.

When the path widened, Corey and May joined Jasmine in the lead.

Corey looked at Jasmine and smiled. "Max picked exactly the right person to lead us. You're doing a great job."

"Thank you." Jasmine smiled back at her friend. "Just like he picked the right person for the small drill team. He really knows what he's doing."

"Although sometimes it doesn't seem like it at first," May said. She was thinking about how she'd had to chase Max all around Pine Hollow while he made up his mind to do exactly what she thought he should.

Jasmine's Christmas Ride

"You guys told me this ride was fun, but you never told me it was this much fun," said Corey.

"And we haven't even gotten to the best part yet," said May.

"But we will soon," said Jasmine. "So you'd better drop back to single file."

"See? I told you she'd be a good leader," May said to Corey. "She knows how to boss us around politely."

Jasmine laughed at her friends, but she never took her eyes off the path. They were coming to a very important part of the trip. Right ahead, the woods opened up into a small meadow. It was wide and flat. Max had told Jasmine that if she thought it was safe, they could trot across the meadow.

Outlaw marched between two pines, and there was the meadow. The stars and moon lit the field more brightly than the string of lights. It was clear and it was smooth. Jasmine decided it would be safe to trot across the well-worn path.

"Prepare to trot!" she called out, then gave her pony the signal. Outlaw immediately began trotting. Jasmine posted, rising ever so slightly in the saddle and then sitting again with every other beat of the trotting gait. She loved to trot

Jasmine's Christmas Ride

on Outlaw. He loved it, too. He moved as if he felt free. She held her lantern high as the others followed.

Jasmine slowed to a walk the instant she reached the woods again. It would be very dangerous to trot under the dark cover of the trees. Even with the lights along the trail, it wouldn't be safe.

"That was great!" she heard riders behind her call. She was glad she'd decided to let everyone trot.

All too soon Jasmine could hear music coming from the center of town. That meant the Starlight Ride was almost over!

On the town green all the people had gathered. The town had decorated the little park with a crèche for Christmas, a menorah for Hanukkah, and a *kinara* for Kwanza. Jasmine had been looking at the decorations ever since they had been put up three weeks earlier. But she didn't think they'd ever looked more beautiful than they did right then. The big Christmas tree in the center of the town glowed brightly.

"Look! Here come the horses!" a little boy called out. Everybody in the crowd turned to watch.

Jasmine lifted her torch a little higher. Outlaw's walk became a bit more of a prance. The riders were about to make their dramatic entrance!

A policeman stood in the street to stop all traffic while the riders crossed to the town green. Hundreds of people—parents, grandparents, brothers, sisters, and anyone else who wanted to be there—greeted the riders. Jasmine's parents stood on the lawn, looking shocked as their daughter led the horses into town. Jasmine grinned at them while her father snapped a picture.

Then, after all the ponies and horses and their riders had joined the crowd, the band began to play holiday music. Everybody joined in to sing.

As she sang the words to "Deck the Halls," Jasmine thought about all the princess pine trees that had lined the path through the woods. When they sang "Hanukkah, O Hanukkah!" she thought about the pretty lights along the way. The last song they sang was "Silent Night." The crowd sang the lullaby softly, and while they sang, Jasmine completed her last job as leader. She took her torch up to the crèche and placed it over the stable.

The crowd burst into applause.

Jasmine's Christmas Ride

When she stepped down, Max brought her a cup of cider. "Merry Christmas, and thank you. You did a wonderful job, Jasmine. I knew you would. You were a good, strong leader. Pine Hollow is lucky to have a rider like you."

She could hardly believe what she was hearing—this on top of the wonderful time she'd had.

"You're welcome," she said softly. "I . . ."

Jasmine wanted to say more to Max. She wanted to tell him that this had been one of the nicest things that had ever happened to her. She wanted to say she'd had more fun leading the Starlight Ride than she would have had on the small drill team. She wanted to promise him that she was going to work hard on the large drill exercise. She wanted to thank him. But when she looked back at him, he was already making his way through the crowd. Four riders wanted to hand him their reins at the same time.

"Merry Christmas!" Jasmine called after him.

"You too!" he said. He smiled warmly at her.

The rest of the evening was a jumble. Everyone was rushing off to family celebrations. Mr. Grover helped the Pony Tails load their ponies onto the trailer and then unload them back at home. Each girl took her own pony home to groom and feed.

Jasmine gave Outlaw a special treat: two carrots, an apple, and three sugar lumps.

She giggled. "Pretend these are goodies from your Christmas stocking!" she said before she hugged him good night. Outlaw seemed very happy. Then Jasmine went inside to sleep and dream about the Starlight Ride one more time.

12 Christmas in the Stable

"Merry Christmas!" Jasmine called to her friends as she rushed into the Grovers' stable the next morning.

May and Corey were already inside, sitting in the straw in an empty stall.

"Doesn't it seem right to have a Pony Tails meeting in a stable at Christmas?" May said to Corey and Jasmine. "I mean, that's where baby Jesus was born—in a stable."

Corey pulled her coat around her and tugged at her hat. "Maybe," she said, but she didn't sound so sure. "It's just so cold outside."

The Pony Tails didn't have much time. Corey was going over to her father's for the afternoon. And there was a lot to talk about before then.

Pony Tails

"Last night was the best night of my life!" Jasmine said, sighing happily. "The only thing missing was the snow."

"There's always next year," Corey said. "Although that was so much fun—maybe we should have a Starlight Ride every night."

"No, one of the best parts about it is that it's just once a year," May said.

"You're probably right about that." Jasmine said, nodding.

"I just knew Max would choose you," Corey said. "The minute he started listing all the qualities the leader was supposed to have, I knew it was you."

"Me too," May said. "Actually, I even tried to ask him to choose you before he did. But he didn't need my help."

"I guess I was the only one who was surprised, then," Jasmine said. "I thought if I wasn't good enough to be on the small drill team, I definitely wouldn't be good enough to lead the ride."

"Of course you're good enough," May said. "We're all good riders. It's just that each of us is better at some things than others."

Corey was nodding. "Like, for instance, I'm better than either of you at one thing."

Jasmine's Christmas Ride

"What's that?" Jasmine asked.

"Well, you're going to have to open these and see." Corey reached into the hay and handed each of them a small, brightly wrapped package.

It took only a few seconds for May and Jasmine to unwrap their bracelets.

"It's just like yours!" May said.

"Yes, except it's got your name and some macaroni on it!" Corey told her.

"And mine has an outlaw's mask!" Jasmine exclaimed.

"I think that means we now have an official Pony Tails bracelet," May said proudly. "We can wear these all the time." She put on her new bracelet. The three girls admired their bracelets together.

"Here's something else for official Pony Tails," Jasmine said, giving each of her friends a medium-sized package.

"I hope it's a binder just like yours," said Corey.

"You peeked!" Jasmine accused her.

"No I didn't!" Corey said. "I'm just hoping." She tore the paper off her present. "This horse looks almost exactly like Samurai!"

"No, it looks like Macaroni!" said May. She

was admiring her own binder. Then she hugged it just the way she liked to hug Macaroni.

"And here's something else for Pony Tails," May said, offering her friends a single large package. Together Jasmine and Corey took the paper off the official Pony Tails scrapbook.

"I put some pictures in it that Dad took of us," May said. "We can keep a record of everything we do. Mom took pictures of all of us last night with an instant camera. I was going to show them to you. Now I'll just put them in the book."

Jasmine smiled as she watched her friend tape photographs of all of them to the next page. Then May wrote "Starlight Ride" underneath the pictures.

"What a great idea!" Jasmine told May. "I can't wait to fill the whole book with stuff from Pony Club and Pony Tails."

"Me either," Corey said. "Thank you, May."

As the three girls flipped through the few pages May had already filled, a wave of happiness swept over Jasmine. She couldn't remember a better or more special Christmas. She loved her friends' gifts, and she'd loved being part of the Starlight Ride.

"Look!" May shouted, pointing out the win-

Jasmine's Christmas Ride

dow of the barn. Both Jasmine and Corey looked where she was pointing.

"Snow! It's really snowing!" Jasmine cried. "I knew it would be a perfect Christmas!"

And they all agreed that it was.

JASMINE'S FAVORITE MOUNTED GAMES

Sometimes it seems as if all we do at Horse Wise is work! But we have lots of fun, too. When we're not practicing drill work, learning how to groom a horse, wrap a sore leg, or muck out a pony's stall, we play mounted games.

Mounted games are games we play on horseback—or ponyback, as we Pony Tails call it. A lot of mounted games are just like regular games with an especially nice twist, because our ponies are playing, too.

Each of the Pony Tails has a favorite type of game. May likes the races best. We do relay

Jasmine's Christmas Ride

races as a team of four members. Sometimes Max lets us invent relay races, like the one where we have to carry an egg on a spoon without breaking it (that's a messy race). There's another where we carry a bucket of water (that's an even messier race). And then there's May's favorite, where we squirt colored ink at a target (that's the messiest of all). Wouldn't you just know that May would like the messiest race the best?

Corey's favorite kind of mounted game is the hunt. At one Horse Wise meeting we had a treasure hunt where we had to follow all kinds of clues to find a treasure. Another time there was a mystery we had to solve on horseback. Max and some of the older riders wrote out clues that we had to decipher to find a missing pony. We found him, too. It doesn't surprise me that Corey likes the kind of game that takes the most thinking. She's very smart.

The ones I like best are the group games. Max showed us how to play shadow tag while we're riding on our ponies. Outlaw is so good that nobody ever makes us It when we play shadow tag. I also love it when we play Simon Says—only, of course, we call it Max Says. There's another game Max showed us that's sort of like musical chairs. The ponies all stand in a circle, facing in. We each have a number, and we're divided into teams, evens and odds. Max calls out a number from each team and a gait, like walk, trot, or canter. If your number is called, you have to back out of the circle and go around as fast as you can at the proper gait. The first rider back to his or her original place wins. If you break your gait and go too fast, you're disqualified. May says I'm the best at that game. Maybe she's right.

We all like playing games, but just because they're fun doesn't mean they aren't hard, too. When we play games, we learn. We have to listen and concentrate and ride our ponies well. Having fun can be work. That's not surprising, though, because it's also true that every time I work hard with my pony, I have fun!

About the Author

Bonnie Bryant was born and raised in New York City, and she still lives there today. She spends her summers in a house on a lake in Massachusetts.

Ms. Bryant began writing about girls and horses when she started The Saddle Club series in 1987. So far there are more than fifty books in that series! Much as she likes telling the stories about Stevie, Carole, and Lisa, she decided that the younger riders at Pine Hollow, notably May Grover, have stories of their own that need telling. That's how Pony Tails was born.

Ms. Bryant rides horses when she has time away from her computer, but she doesn't have a horse of her own. She likes to ride different horses and enjoys a variety of riding experiences. She says she thinks most of her readers are much better riders than she is!

this book belongs to

caitlin monast

Photo by Robert Cushman Hayes

02-29323-0